KNIGHT QUEST

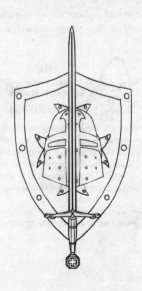

First published in Great Britain by HarperCollins *Children's Books* in 2013
HarperCollins *Children's Books* is a division of HarperCollins*Publishers* Ltd,
77-85 Fulham Palace Road, Hammersmith, London, W6 8JB.

The HarperCollins website address is: www.harpercollins.co.uk

1

Text © Hothouse Fiction Limited 2013
Illustrations © HarperCollins *Children's Books* 2013
Illustrations by Dynamo

ISBN 978-0-00-794085-1

Printed and bound in England by Clays Ltd, St Ives plc

MIX
Paper from
responsible sources
FSC **FSC® C007454**
www.fsc.org

FSC™ is a non-profit international organisation established to promote
the responsible management of the world's forests. Products carrying the
FSC label are independently certified to assure consumers that they come
from forests that are managed to meet the social, economic and
ecological needs of present and future generations,
and other controlled sources.

Find out more about HarperCollins and the environment at
www.harpercollins.co.uk/green

CHRIS BLAKE

TiME HUNTERS

KNIGHT QUEST

HarperCollins *Children's Books*

Travel through time with Tom and Isis
on more

adventures!

CONTENTS

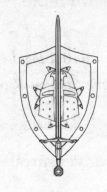

With special thanks to
Marnie Stanton-Riches

PROLOGUE

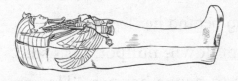

Five thousand years ago

Princess Isis and her pet cat, Cleo, stood outside the towering carved gates to the Afterlife. It had been rotten luck to fall off a pyramid and die at only ten years of age, but Isis wasn't worried – the Afterlife was meant to be great. People were dying to go there, after all! Her mummy's wrappings were so uncomfortable she couldn't wait a second longer to get in, get her body back and wear normal clothes again.

"Oi, Aaanuuubis, Anubidooby!" Isis shouted impatiently. "When you're ready, you old dog!"

Cleo started to claw Isis's shoulder. Then she yowled, jumping from Isis's arms and cowering behind her legs.

"Calm down, fluffpot," Isis said, bending to stroke her pet. "He can't exactly woof me to death!" The princess laughed, but froze when she stood up. Now she understood what Cleo had been trying to tell her.

Looming up in front of her was the enormous jackal-headed god of the Underworld himself, Anubis. He was so tall that Isis's neck hurt to look up at him. He glared down his long snout at her with angry red eyes. There was nothing pet-like about him. Isis gulped.

"'WHEN YOU'RE READY, YOU OLD DOG?'" Anubis growled. "'ANUBIDOOBY?'"

Isis gave the god of the Underworld a winning smile and held out five shining amulets. She had been buried with them so she could give them to Anubis to gain entry to the Afterlife. There was a sixth amulet too – a gorgeous green one. But Isis had hidden it under her arm. Green *was* her favourite colour, and surely Anubis didn't need all six.

Except the god didn't seem to agree. His fur bristled in rage. "FIVE? Where is the sixth?" he demanded.

Isis shook her head. "I was only given five," she said innocently.

To her horror, Anubis grabbed the green amulet from its hiding place. "You little LIAR!" he bellowed.

Thunder started to rumble. The ground shook. Anubis snatched all six amulets and tossed them into the air. With a loud crack and a flash of lightning, they vanished.

"You hid them from me!" he boomed. "Now I have hidden them from you – in the most dangerous places throughout time."

Isis's bandaged shoulders drooped in despair. "So I c-c-can't come into the Afterlife then?"

"Not until you have found each and every

one. But first, you will have to get out of this..." Anubis clicked his fingers. A life-sized pottery statue of the goddess Isis, whom Isis was named after, appeared before him.

Isis felt herself being sucked into the statue, along with Cleo. "What are you doing to me?" she yelled.

"You can only escape if somebody breaks the statue," Anubis said. "So you'll have plenty of time to think about whether trying to trick the trickster god himself was a good idea!"

The walls of the statue closed around Isis, trapping her and Cleo inside. The sound of Anubis's evil laughter would be the last sound they would hear for a long, long time...

CHAPTER 1
CLASS CLOWN

"I'm going to have *such* fun going through your things when you're at school," Isis said, rubbing her ragged hands together. "Your computer. Your football-sticker book. Your Star Wars figures."

Tom dropped his school bag on the floor. "NO WAY!"

Mum put her hand on his forehead. "Are you feeling all right, dear? I only asked you if you had your lunch box. There's no need to have a fit."

Tom glanced over at the stairs, where the mummified figure of Princess Isis Amun-Ra was sitting. Her cat, Cleo, also wrapped in bandages, was curled up on her lap, invisible to everyone except Tom. Isis's crumbly old wrappings had left ancient white dust all over the carpet.

"Have fun at school!" she said. Waving stiffly, she picked up Cleo and started to shuffle off to *his* room.

It wasn't fair! No one else in Tom's class was beginning the new term knowing that the mummies of an Ancient Egyptian princess and her pet cat were at their home, snooping around and generally causing havoc. Mum and Dad couldn't see Isis and Cleo, so if the mummies made a mess, Tom knew he would get the blame.

"I'll just fetch your P.E. kit," Mum said, disappearing into the kitchen.

Tom rounded on Isis. "Listen! You mustn't touch anything while I'm out. We don't know when Anubis will send us on our next mission. So..." He scratched his shock of blond curls as he searched for the right words, "...just keep out of trouble."

Isis leaned over the banister. "Don't get all bossy with me. You're the whole reason I'm here. It was you who smashed my statue at your dad's museum. *You* set me free again. Remember?"

Tom threw his hands in the air. "Yes, but aren't you forgetting the bit where I risked my neck travelling back in time to help you find your first amulet? It was *you* who tried to trick Anubis by keeping one of the amulets for yourself, but now *I'm* the one who's been roped into babysitting a dead princess and her cat!"

Isis made a huffing noise and tossed her head back with a crack. "There are still five amulets left to find. And until Anubis sends us on our next challenge, I might as well enjoy myself. So if *you* won't entertain me, I'll make my own fun." She poked herself in the chest and accidentally put her finger right through her crusty ribs.

Cleo mewed in agreement and pawed at the banister spindles.

There was no way Tom was going to let Isis rummage through his belongings. There was only one thing for it.

"Look, just get in the car, will you?" Tom groaned. "You'll have to come to school with me."

Tom sat at his desk and looked down at Cleo, who was curled up asleep underneath his chair.

"Fun holiday?" Tom's classmate Jodie asked him.

"Oh, it was out of this world," Tom said, smiling. "Literally."

But he stopped smiling pretty quickly

when he saw what Isis was doing. She was wandering round the room, fiddling with everything. She looked over at Tom.

"This is much more fun than being cooped up in your boring house," she shouted above the noise of the chattering children.

Tom looked around. Nobody seemed to have noticed the fact that the globe had started spinning on its own, or that the cold tap had just turned itself on and off. But how long would that last?

He got out of his seat and went to the front of the room, pretending that he needed to sharpen his pencil. "Can't you just sit quietly somewhere and stop messing with things?" he whispered to Isis over the noise of the pencil sharpener.

When Tom returned to his seat, Isis sat down on the windowsill, crossed her bony, bandaged legs and started to leaf through the pages of a book. This time, the teacher, Mr Braintree, noticed.

"Shut that window, James!" Mr Braintree shouted to the boy sitting closest to Isis.

James looked at the window and screwed up his face. "But it is shut, sir."

The teacher pushed his glasses up his nose and frowned. "There must be a draft. I'll have to report it to the caretaker. I can't have books flapping around. It's very distracting."

For a full five minutes, Isis sat still. Tom started to relax, but then Mr Braintree began to take the register.

Isis jumped off the windowsill, shuffled stiffly to the front of the class and stood behind Mr Braintree.

Oh no! What is she going to do now? Tom wondered.

When he noticed Isis drawing a rude
cartoon of Anubis on the whiteboard,
he faked a coughing fit to distract
her.

Isis shuffled over to him and thumped him
on the back.

In between coughs, Tom hissed, "Look,
Isis, if you don't stop messing around, I won't
help you find the next amulet. And then
you'll never get into the Afterlife."

Isis sat down at an empty desk with a deep sigh. She folded her arms and managed to keep still for the rest of the lesson.

Finally, the bell for morning break went. Tom pushed Cleo and Isis into the playground as quickly as possible.

"Aren't you coming to play footy?" Tom's friends Rav and Danny asked.

"Not today, guys," Tom said, herding Isis and Cleo towards a quiet spot behind the art block. When they reached the secluded triangle of trees, he breathed a sigh of relief and sat down on the grass.

"At last! A break from your nonsense!" he said to Isis.

But Isis had already begun to climb one of the trees. She pulled herself onto a thick bough and sat with her legs dangling just above Tom's head.

"Oh, come on," she laughed, wiggling her mouldy toes. "I was just having fun. Don't be such a spoilsport."

Tom tugged at some clover in the grass. "I wonder where we'll go next time. Do you think Anubis will come back soon?"

"He'd better get a move on," Isis said. "Princesses don't like being kept waiting."

"He's a god. You shouldn't be so impatient," Tom said.

But he had scarcely finished speaking when the playground beneath them started to tremble.

Tom scrambled to his feet. "Oh, you're kidding!" he cried. "Not here!"

Tom looked round to find the source of the rumbling. Sure enough, a huge doggy snout pushed through the leaves just above Isis's head.

Isis yelped as she was shoved off the bough by the giant, jackal-headed god. She landed with a thump on the ground next to Tom.

"Are you ready for your next quest?" Anubis boomed down at them.

His pointed ears poked through the leaves of the tree. Tom looked at Anubis's giant teeth, which were yellowing and sharp. Then he gazed into the god's angry red eyes and felt terror tingle along his spine.

In their first mission Tom had nearly met his death at the hands of Ancient Rome's fiercest gladiator. What deadly challenge would they face *this* time? Would he get out alive?

"Cat got your tongue?" Anubis asked, growling slightly.

"More like *dog* got your tongue," Isis whispered at Tom's side.

Tom heard shouts from the playground.

He remembered that it was double Maths next. Snore-tastic! Even though the next challenge was bound to be dangerous, a trip through time sounded much better than fractions with Mr Braintree.

"You bet we're ready," Tom said.

He took Isis's hand, and they each held one of Cleo's paws, making a circle. The wind started to whip up around them and Tom felt himself being pulled through the tunnels of space and time...

CHAPTER 2
PIGGING OUT

"Aargh!" Tom shouted, flailing his arms and legs as he plummeted to the ground.

Thump, thump, flump!

Tom, Isis and Cleo landed heavily in some long grass.

"Where are we?" Isis asked.

Tom peered at the towering trees that surrounded them. He could hear the sound of flowing water in the distance. "I've no idea," he said. He pointed to Isis and Cleo. "Look! You've got your normal bodies back again!"

Cleo mewed, sat in the grass and started to lick the stripy fur on her outstretched hind leg.

Isis prodded her tummy through the rough woollen tunic she was now wearing. She beamed at Tom. "That's more like it!" she said. She stroked her plaits and fluttered the lashes of her kohled eyes.

Tom watched Isis's fingers play over the folds of the heavy grey cloak that hung from her shoulders. Her smile had vanished.

"What is this *ghastly* scratchy thing?" she cried. She sniffed it cautiously. "It smells like a wet dog. Eeuw."

Examining the brooch that fastened his own cloak, Tom said, "See this?" He pointed to the tiny bronze serpents that twisted together in a beautiful tangle. "Dad's got this kind of thing in his museum. They're from the Early Middle Ages."

Tom was struck by an idea. "Are you still wearing your ring?" he said.

Isis looked at her hand and nodded. "Good thinking," she said. With her other hand, she touched the gold ring in the shape of a scarab. On it was a hieroglyph of her namesake, the Egyptian goddess Isis.

"Help us, oh Isis. Give us guidance, oh goddess of magic and children," she said.

Out from the ring floated the silvery prophecy, which Tom read aloud to Isis.

"*In cavernous lair the dragons lie*
In wait for the foolish and brave.
Come show your mettle, though you may die,
Be you honourable knight or knave.
If it's treasure you seek, the king's the man
You need to see applaud.
Seek challenge where the legend began,
Find a stone within a sword."

The silvery words blew away on the breeze.

Tom scratched his head. "I've heard of the sword in the stone but not the other way round."

Isis stroked a meowing Cleo. "Go on, Professor Smartypants. Tell me and Fluffpot all about it."

Tom tried to hide his smile. "Well, back in the fifth century there was this boy called Arthur, right? He was the only person able to pull out a sword that was stuck in a lump of stone. That meant he was the true King of England."

Isis folded her arms. "What a silly way to pick your ruler!" she scoffed.

"Stop interrupting!" Tom said. "So, King Arthur was really big on chivalry and honour. His knights were noble, brave men.

The king chose them to fight for him. They wore some pretty cool armour, with colourful coats of arms on their tunics and cloaks."

He remembered the medieval chain mail on display in Dad's museum. "And they sat at a round table!"

Tom thought for a moment. "The riddle makes it sound like we need to become one of King Arthur's knights to find the amulet."

Isis raised an eyebrow. "It also mentions knaves. *Be you honourable knight or knave.* Maybe we could become one of those instead?"

"A knave is an old-fashioned word for an unkind, dishonest person," Tom explained, frowning.

"Well, that's no good. We'll just have to become knights then," Isis said decisively.

But that seemed impossible to Tom, when

he remembered stories about the Knights of the Round Table's heroic deeds. How could two kids possibly become knights?

"The riddle also mentions dragons," said Isis. "I've always wanted to see a real, live dragon. Do you think we'll be battling against them?" she asked.

Tom scuffed the ground with his foot. "That's the bit I don't understand," he aid. "Everybody knows dragons weren't real."

Isis giggled. "Of course they were real. I saw dragons painted on the walls back in Egypt. How could the scribes have painted them if they hadn't seen them? Duh!"

Tom was suddenly distracted by the thunder of hooves behind them. A boy riding a large chestnut horse galloped into view. He was carrying a long, pointed stick

31

in one hand, like a lance. As the boy drew alongside them, the stick slipped and poked Isis on the arm.

"OUCH!" she shrieked and grabbed at her shoulder. Shaking her fist, Isis started to run after the boy. "Hey, you! How DARE you poke me! Come back here at once!"

The boy reined in his horse and sprang out of the saddle. He was dressed in tight, grotty trousers and a mud-streaked brown tunic that looked like it had been made from a sack. There was a rope tied round his waist. Tom thought he smelled like Mum's compost heap.

"Oh, my word! I'm so, so sorry!" the boy said, bowing. "Did I catch you with my stick?

Oh, my lady, a thousand apologies." He turned to Tom and offered his hand. "I'm Alymere," he said. "Al for short."

Tom looked warily at Al's filthy hand but shook it anyway.

"I'm Tom. This is Isis and her cat, Cleo," he explained. "We're travellers. We're just passing through. Could you tell us where we are?"

"Oh, well, you're on the farm where I work," Al said, treating them to a welcoming smile. His teeth may have been rotten, but he looked very friendly. "I'm a pig-boy."

Isis pointed at Al's stick. "And does your job involve poking strangers with pointy sticks? Surely you didn't mistake me for a pig," she said stroppily.

Al blushed. "Sorry again, my beautiful lady," he said. "You look nothing like a pig."

Isis smiled and patted her hair. "Well, then, no harm done."

"But I was practising my knightly skills, see?" explained Al. He looked down at his muddy boots. "One day, I'm going to be one of King Arthur's knights."

"King Arthur?" Tom gasped.

Al grinned again. "The one and only. He's coming to the village today."

Tom felt his heart beat faster as he remembered the words of the riddle. He looked over at Isis and winked.

"*The king's the man*, eh?" he said.

Isis nodded eagerly. "Yes! Tell us more! It sounds dreadfully exciting."

Al mounted his horse and turned to the three travellers. "You lot must be thirsty. Why don't you come to my hut for some mead and I'll tell you all about it."

Al's hut was shabby, with a patchy, thatched roof and a smouldering fire in the corner. Tom and Isis sat on the floor and listened to Al's grand plan.

"I've been practising to be a knight for years," the pig-boy explained, reclining on his bed of straw. "Then I heard King Arthur was visiting today. It's my big chance! I borrowed that horse there from my cousin, Philbert. He's a lovely beast, he is. The horse... not Philbert!"

Tom looked out at the plump horse that was busy munching grass outside. *He doesn't look like he can gallop very fast*, Tom thought. "He looks... er... solid," he said, nodding.

Al swigged from his flagon of mead. "Aye. He's called Acorn. I gave him that name because I've been trying this trick where I pick up things from the ground while we're riding." Al grinned. "At first it was big stuff like this flagon here, or a turnip. Now I can pick up a single acorn when we're galloping at full speed."

His words were drowned out by a terrible din coming from outside. A herd of squealing pigs stampeded past the hut.

"Oh no!" Al wailed. "My pigs must have escaped from the field."

Tom jumped to his feet and followed Al outside. "Don't worry," he shouted above the noise. "We'll help you catch them, won't we, Isis?"

Isis looked uncertainly at the fat, pink animals. "We will?"

"Let's see who can catch the most!" Tom challenged.

"You're on!" she said.

When they had rounded up all the pigs,

Isis was plastered head to toe in mud. "Look at the state of me!" she wailed. Then she grinned at Tom. "At least I rounded up more pigs than you did!"

Al scratched his head. "Stumped if I know how they got out," he said.

Just then, a young man with neatly brushed, long hair strolled past. He tossed a rich blue velvet cloak over his shoulder with

a flourish, and kicked Cleo out of the way
with a fine leather boot as he stopped just
outside Al's hut and snapped his fingers.

"Hey, pig-boy!" he called. "Keep your
animals under control in future. They've
almost ruined my father's garden."

Wringing his hands, Al said, "I'm so sorry,
sir. I have no idea how they escaped."

"I opened the gate to get to my horse,"

the man said in a haughty voice. "My family owns this field, after all. It's not my fault if your pigs run all over the place."

"Sorry, sir. Yes, sir," Al mumbled.

The rude young man looked round the hut, disdain on his face. He brushed a cobweb off his shoulder and said, "Ugh. I hate spiders. This place is only fit for a pig... or a pig-boy!" With a shudder, he turned on his heel and stomped off.

"Who was *that*?" Tom asked.

"Percival, the squire's son," Al said.

"Why were you so nice to him?" Isis asked, picking up Cleo and giving her a cuddle. "He was vile!"

Al sighed and rolled his eyes. "I know. But if I don't keep in the squire's good books, I could lose my job." He poked glumly at a hole in his boot. "My dreams don't count for anything in this village. Folks like Percival and his father... as far as they're concerned, I'm just the lowest of the low."

"Well, they can all go and stick their heads in a pile of pig poo, because you're going to be a knight," Isis said, wiping her dirty hands on Tom. "And we're going to help you."

Tom nodded. "Yeah. Today's your lucky day," he said. "Let's go and meet King Arthur!"

CHAPTER 3
THE REAL KING ARTHUR

"I can't believe we're going to meet the real King Arthur," Tom said. "I mean, *really* real!" He punched the air with excitement.

As they followed Al and Acorn through a tunnel of lush, green trees, Tom drank in the mossy woodland smell. In his mind's eye, he was already lost in his own medieval adventure, riding through the forest with King Arthur and the Knights of the Round Table.

"What do you mean, *really* real?" Isis said, walking carefully with the hem of her cloak gathered in her hands.

"Well, there are lots of stories about him," Tom said. "But there's nothing to prove he ever actually existed."

"The Egyptians didn't need to make up kings to tell good stories," Isis said, tripping on a loose rock. She tutted loudly. "Our roads were better too."

Presently, the dense woodland came to an end. Tom could see small thatched huts dotted about on the edges of a grassy clearing.

Al turned round, flashing them his crooked smile. "We're here." He pointed to a large building that was open on all sides.

"This is the
meeting place."

"*Make way!*"

Tom leaped to one side as two burly
villagers stumbled past him. They were
carrying a heavy-looking table and pushing
through the gathering crowd.

"I want to sit there," Isis said, pointing
to a large, beautifully carved chair at the
very front.

"Listen, the
people here have come
to see the king, not a ten-year-
old girl," Tom said. "You'll have to stand
at the back with the rest of us lowly mortals."

He was getting jostled on all sides by villagers trying to claim the best spot.

"Out of the way, pig-boy!" a man in a fine linen tunic with a velvet cloak said to Al. He pushed Al aside so roughly that the boy bumped into another wealthy-looking villager.

"Oi! Pig-boy! You stink," the second man said, holding his nose.

Tom saw Al gulp and bow. "So sorry, sir. I did take a bath last week."

Stepping away from the man, Al accidentally stepped on Percival's shiny boots.

"You clumsy oaf," Percival hissed, glaring. "You're not even fit to clean my boots, pig-boy."

"Yeah, why did *you* even bother coming?" the second man said, sneering at Al. "Haven't you got pigs to tend?"

"Here! You leave young Alymere be!" an old woman shouted. She slammed the basket full of clothes that she was holding on to the ground.

The mean man looked down his nose at the woman. "I don't need a lesson in manners from a washerwoman, thank you *very* much," he said.

Tom pulled Isis aside. "These villagers are a pretty nasty bunch, aren't they?" he said.

Isis nodded. "I know. I hate to see people looking down their noses at the likes of Al, just because he's poor," she said.

"Oh, really?" Tom asked, chuckling. "And *you're* not a bit snooty, are you?"

"*Me?*" Isis squeaked. "I'm not like *them!*" Her eyes widened. "Am I?"

"Ooh, just a teensy bit!" Tom said.

Isis blushed and looked at her feet. "It's a princess thing," she muttered. "We're used to getting our own way. I don't mean to be nasty…"

"I know." Tom said. But sometimes I feel a bit like Al around you."

Suddenly a fanfare of horns rang throughout the meeting place.

"Listen! They're coming!" Tom said, beaming with anticipation. "I can't believe we're going to see King Arthur with our own eyes."

The sound of jangling reins, clopping hooves and snorting horses could be heard getting closer. When Tom finally got a glimpse of the king's party, he gasped at the troop of impressive-looking men riding enormous horses.

"Look at those big, beefy guys," he said. "I bet they're bodyguards." Tom marvelled at the broadswords swinging in scabbards at their sides. The men were wearing gold-stitched cloaks and sitting in saddles bearing colourful coats of arms.

"Amazing," Tom breathed.

Finally, a grey stallion trotted into the centre of the meeting place. Everyone moved aside to let its rider through. They all knelt on one knee on the ground.

"Hail the King!" the villagers shouted.

King Arthur leaped down from his saddle. He stood by the carved chair, surrounded by the sea of kneeling villagers. In place of the grand, strapping giant that Tom had expected, he saw a disappointingly short, bearded man. The king wore just a simple white tunic and dark trousers beneath a travel cloak that was utterly plain, apart from a narrow trim of white fur. His hair was short, messy and blond, rather like Dad's. He wasn't even wearing a crown.

"Gather round!" he said in a booming voice that seemed to make the entire village stand to attention.

A smile spread across Tom's face. *Now* he realised why this ordinary-looking man was a legendary hero. He could feel admiration pouring from everyone around him, as they hung on to the king's every word.

King Arthur cleared his throat. "What a fine and pleasant land God has given me to rule! Look at you, my admirable subjects," he said, spreading his arms wide.

Everyone smiled.

King Arthur clenched his fist and thumped his chest.

51

"The sturdy, noble-hearted people of England are the envy of the world. Our green pastures and glorious forests are closer to heaven than any other realm."

The villagers began to clap and whistle.

King Arthur held his hand high. "But wait! Even as I speak to you, there are tribes in Germany hatching plans of great evil."

The horrified villagers gasped, like party balloons losing their air.

"SAXONS!" King Arthur shouted.

He said the word with such disgust in his voice that the room erupted into a frenzy of loud booing.

"Saxons have a mind to sail here and take this blessed land as their own. But I have every faith that even the humblest English farmhand will protect his home fearlessly."

There was a rumble of agreement

throughout the crowd.

"And that is why I am here – I'm looking to recruit one more knight to my round table." King Arthur flicked his cloak back and put his hand on the hilt of his sword. "Men of my country, if you believe that you can defend our land, if you have a horse, and you think you are brave, then step forward now and take the challenges I set you. Remember! I will bestow this special knighthood on one man only – the winner!"

Tom and Isis exchanged glances. This was their big chance to become *honorourable knights* and find the amulet.

"Me! Me! I'm brave!" a young lad shouted. "I'll fight for King and country."

"Me too!"

A throng of men surged towards King Arthur.

53

"Come on," said Al, beckoning Tom and Isis towards him. "Let's get in the queue before it's too late."

Isis's nose shot into the air so fast that her headband almost fell off. "Queuing? Pah! Princesses don't queue. I'm going straight to the front," she said, marching off.

Tom grabbed her by her elbow and pulled her back. "Hey! You're in England now!" he said. "People wait their turn here." He lowered his voice to a whisper. "Even Ancient Egyptian princesses."

Tom pointed to Percival, who had barged to the front.

"You're not like him, are you?" Tom asked.

"No, definitely not," Isis said.

With a sigh, she followed Tom to the back of the queue. She grimaced and wrinkled her nose. Cleo coughed and spluttered like she was choking on a furball. But queue they did – surrounded by villagers who smelled of everything from woodsmoke to sweaty feet.

Next to Al, however, stood a tall villager, who was clearly wealthy. His clothes were fine. The hilt of his sword was decorated with rubies. His teeth were almost white! The villager looked down at Al as though he was a bogey on the end of his nose.

Poking Al in the shoulder, he said, "Do you honestly think King Arthur is going to give a smelly pig-boy a second look?"

Tom watched Al's cheeks turn red. Al looked at his feet.

"And didn't you know you have to have a horse?" the snooty villager said.

Al looked up and grinned. "Oh, well,

that's not a problem. I've got a horse; he's called Acorn."

Tom and Isis nodded at Al encouragingly.

The man snorted. "Can you imagine what that animal looks like?" he said, slapping his thigh. "We'll have to call you Sir Stinkalot on his valiant charger, Dobbin!" He burst into peals of nasty laughter.

Isis stood on her tiptoes and stared angrily into the villager's face. "Ooh, you sneering, snotty, stuck-up…" she snarled between gritted teeth.

Tom could see Isis was so full of rage, she could hardly choose which insults to hurl at the man first.

"I'm going to make you wish you hadn't said those nasty things!" Isis shouted, aiming a kick at his leg.

The man was glaring down at her now.

His hand was raised, ready to cuff her ear.
Then he seemed to think better of it.

"I know," he said. "Perhaps a day or two
in the stocks, having
rotten vegetables
and stones thrown
at you, will teach
you how to
behave.

Or, better still, I could arrange for you to have a go on the ducking stool. Yes! A plunge in the freezing river will cool you down. If you drown, at least we'll know you weren't possessed by demons. Hee hee hee! And if you live... why! We can burn you!"

The man reached out and grabbed Isis by her cloak.

"Put my friend down, you big bully!" Tom said.

Cleo hissed and scratched at the man.

"*That's* not how a nobleman's supposed to behave!" Al said, clearly horrified. "You let go of my friend now, sir, or I'll... I'll challenge you to a duel!" He slapped his fist against the palm of his hand.

The nasty villager, however, seemed to be enjoying himself too much to take Al's threat seriously. "Out of my way, Sir Stinkalot!" he said, pushing Al aside.

Isis kicked out and wriggled. "Let go of me, you ugly old man!" she cried.

But no matter how hard she struggled, the man would not let her go.

CHAPTER 4
IT'S A KNOCK OUT

Tom heard a growl that sounded like it
was coming from a tiger... but looked
down and saw it was really coming from
a little striped cat. Cleo hissed at the man
holding her mistress and sank her teeth into
his leg.

"Ow!" shrieked the man, dropping Isis.

"Serves you right, you big bully," said Isis,
scooping up Cleo and stroking her fur.

★

"Gather round, men!" King Arthur shouted.

Tom, Isis and Al were standing among the group of would-be knights that had assembled in a grassy clearing.

Tom whispered in Isis's ear. "It was brave of you to stand up to such a meany, but next time think before you start hurling insults at people. No wonder you got into so much trouble with Anubis!"

Isis swirled her cloak regally over her shoulder. "A princess can say whatever she wants."

"Shh!" Tom said. "Right now, you're a boy, trying out to become a knight. Got it?"

King Arthur beckoned everyone to him. "Come closer!"

They all shuffled forward so that even the men standing at the back could hear the king's deep, rich voice.

"To sort the true knights from the lily-livered hopefuls, there will be a series of contests," King Arthur said. "First, we will have shooting, then lances, and finally sword fighting. You may choose your preferred method of combat, but you must supply your own weapons. We will begin in ten minutes."

Tom thought about the armoury in the medieval room of Dad's museum. There were bows and arrows, swords, lances and spiked maces. Tom loved the shining suits of armour that knights wore, along with shields and tunics of chain mail that covered the head as well as the body.

"Knights fought with some really brilliant, deadly weapons," Tom said to Isis. "But we're unarmed!"

Al turned to them, grinning with delight.

"So, what are you two going to make, then?" he asked.

"MAKE?" Tom cried. "I'm rubbish at arts and crafts."

"Don't fret, Tom!" Al said. "I'll help you pick a nice, sturdy tree branch. Makes a smashing lance, see? There's nothing to it!" He turned to Isis. "What about you?"

Isis picked up five or six sharp pieces of flint from the ground. "I know exactly what I'm going to make," she said. First she cut a small triangle of leather from the top of her boots. Then she tore three strips of cloth from the hem of her tunic and plaited them together.

Al clapped his hands. "A slingshot! What a cracking idea, Isis! Are you any good?"

"Good?" Isis said. "I was taught to use one of these when I was just five by a general in

my father's army. I can bring down a fast
hare at a hundred paces!"

Al whistled in awe. Tom rolled his eyes.
But Isis just strutted off to join those who
were taking part in the shooting trial.

King Arthur blew a horn and held his hand
high. "The test of your shooting skills will
be a knock-out round. Contestants may use
a bow and arrow or a sling. If you get shot,
you're out. First, we'll have the short lad
with black hair and that fine gentleman." He
pointed to Isis and then to the man who had

complained that Al was stinky.

"BEGIN!" commanded King Arthur.

Tom watched as Isis wedged a chunk of flint inside the leather triangle.

She laughed and said, "Brace yourself, Lord Bullypants!"

Before the man could even raise his bow, Isis whizzed her sling round twice and released her stone. It sped across the clearing... *thunk!*... and found its mark. The villager clutched at his foot and started to hop around.

"Ow!" he said.

Isis pretended to sniff the air. "Does anyone else smell that?" she said, grinning at Al. "The sweet scent of victory!"

One by one, King Arthur sent forward villagers to duel against Isis. She was a crack shot. Each man ended up clutching at bruised ribs, arms and legs.

Isis looked over at King Arthur to see if he was watching.

Sure enough, he was staring straight at her!

"Pretty good, yes?" she boasted, aiming at an archer, who was sprinting and tumbling round the clearing to avoid being hit by her.

But suddenly Isis pulled back her sling and the fabric ripped.

"AARGH! USELESS!" she shouted in frustration. "These bits of cloth aren't fit to line a bird's nest!" Isis threw her sling onto the ground and stamped on it. She felt a heavy hand on her shoulder and turned round.

"King Arthur!" she said.

He looked down at her and shook his head solemnly. "You're a great shot, youngster, but my knights need to keep a cool head – even if the flames of hell itself should lick at their feet."

"But—" Isis said.

"DISQUALIFIED!" King Arthur shouted.

Isis stomped off to the sidelines, her face red with shame.

King Arthur called the lancers next – now it was Tom's go!

"Best of three!" the king announced. "READY…"

Tom stood with a thundering heart, facing

the stocky man on the opposite side of the clearing. The branch that Al had chosen for him was far heavier than any cricket bat Tom had picked up.

"SET…"

The muscles in his arms quivered, but Tom ignored them.

"CHARGE!" King Arthur cried.

"Aaaargh!" Tom growled.

Mustering every ounce of strength he had, he sprinted towards his opponent. The harder he ran, the quicker the other man's lance came at him. But Tom didn't flinch.

Doof!

Tom took a punch in the belly from his opponent's lance. He doubled up, feeling Al's mead sloshing about angrily in his stomach.

Tom stood up quickly, readying himself

for another charge. He had two more
chances left.

"You can be a knight, Tom," he muttered
under his breath. "Be brave. Show no
weakness." By now, though, the muscles in
his arm were really aching.

Once again,
Tom sprinted
at the man
opposite him.
Clonk! His lance
started to trail on the
ground. *Clonk-a-donk!*
He stumbled and
tripped.

King Arthur blew
his horn. "Stop the
duel!" he cried.

He marched up to Tom and took the branch from him. "I see you have the heart of a lion, young man. But I need knights that are strong enough to bear their lances through a full day's hard riding."

Tom groaned.

"DISQUALIFIED!"

Tom joined Isis on the sidelines.

"Poor Sir Smartypants," she teased. "Shame they don't have a fact-spouting duel. You'd *definitely* win that."

"Oh, thanks!" said Tom.

Isis sighed and patted his arm. "It was just a joke. You weren't too bad, all right?"

"You weren't too bad, either," said Tom. "But right now Al's our only hope of getting close to a knight. And it's a knight we need, if we're going to find the amulet. So let's cheer him on."

The remaining contestants had all chosen to fight with swords. There were so many of them that King Arthur split them into two groups.

"Take that! Whoops! Sorry, sir! And that!" Al cried, using a sword made from a stout stick. He parried and nimbly sidestepped the blows that came from men much bigger than him. At every turn, Al darted forward and thrust his sword at his opponents until they were defeated.

"Go, Al!" Tom and Isis shouted.

Even Cleo purred loudly in support.

Al continued to knock out contestants, all the while politely apologising for any harm he was causing. Soon, the villagers started to cheer him on too.

"He's brilliant!" Tom said. "All that

practice really paid off! You've got to be as strong as a bear to carry one of those broadswords."

Isis shrugged. "I suppose if you can lug barrels full of water and swill to a pig's trough all day, you can lift just about anything," she said.

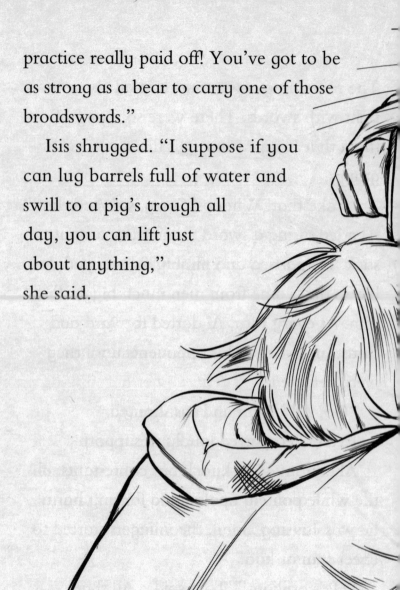

Tom glanced over to the other group and groaned. "Oh, no!" he said. "Posing Percival's still standing too. You know what's going to happen, don't you?"

Isis nodded. "Al's going to have to duel against him."

CHAPTER 5
HORSING AROUND

Al and Percival stood side by side before King Arthur. Both were out of breath, but every other would-be knight had either keeled over with exhaustion, been disqualified or been injured.

"The final challenge shall be on horseback," King Arthur told the crowd. "Fetch your mounts!" he boomed to the two young men.

Al hurried over to Tom and Isis, wiping his brow with his grimy rope belt, leaving a smear of dirt across his forehead. Al glanced over at Percival, who still looked immaculate in his fine clothes and shiny boots.

"Oh, Lord. How can a simple lad like me hope to win against a nobleman?" he said.

"Don't worry," said Tom. "Just because Percival's got a title doesn't mean he's any better than you."

"Too right," agreed Isis. "You're just as good as any noble."

Al smiled at his new friends and went to fetch Acorn.

"Do you really think he's got a chance?" asked Isis.

"We'd better hope so. Here he comes now!" Tom said excitedly.

Al entered the clearing at a trot, bobbing

proudly up and down in the saddle. He
waved as he spotted Tom, Isis and Cleo
among the spectators, and cantered over to
where they were standing.

"What on earth is under your saddle?" Isis said, pointing to the grubby green-and-red cloth that hung over Acorn's flanks.

Al grinned. "He looks right dashing with that, doesn't he?" he said. "It's like one of those silk saddlecloths with knightly coats of arms on, only, get this…" He leaned down and whispered, "it's a bit of an old blanket really. You wouldn't know, would you?"

"Well, ye—" Isis began.

Tom clapped his hand over her mouth. "No, Al. You'd never know, *would you*, Isis? It's really smart."

"Thing is," Al said, suddenly seeming gloomy, "that Percival's going to gallop in on a thoroughbred charger. And I didn't want old Acorn, here, with his fluffy, feathery old hooves, to feel scruffy."

Sure enough, an 'Ooooh' rippled through

the crowd of villagers as Percival rode in on a tall, black stallion. Tom couldn't help but gasp at Percival's shining suit of armour and the horse's gleaming tack.

"What an idiot!" Isis said. "He looks like he's about to lead an army into battle, not duel with a boy on a carthorse."

She folded her arms and scowled. "I really can't stand show offs!"

Tom looked sideways at her and laughed. "*You* can't stand show offs?"

Percival sat smugly in his grand saddle, with the visor on his helmet raised up so they could see him smirk. He whispered into his stallion's ear and made clicking noises.

Suddenly the horse began to prance round the clearing. Percival steered the horse up close to the villagers, so they could have a better view. The horse flicked its tail in a peasant woman's face.

"Aargh!" she cried, dropping the wicker basket that she had been holding. "Oh no, my eggs!" The woman started to pick up what she could from the yellow, yolky mess on the ground.

Percival just laughed and trotted away.

But Al jumped down from Acorn and helped the woman gather the unbroken eggs back into her basket.

"No need to fret, my good lady," Al said to the woman. "There's still a few that will make it into your pan."

The woman smiled and patted Al on the arm. "You're a good lad. I hope you put that horrid Percival in his place."

"Now for the joust!" King Arthur announced. "These lances are *deadly* weapons. The stakes are high!"

Tom watched as King Arthur took two heavy-looking lances with shining, carved hilts from his servants and passed one each to the contestants.

"Which of you will show the kind of courage I am looking for?" Arthur asked.

Al sat astride Acorn's broad back,

looking slightly sick as he stared down at the gleaming lance.

"Al's strong and knows his stuff, but I hope a real lance isn't too different from a homemade one," Tom said.

"Posing Percy seems to be struggling with the weight of his," Isis said. "All the fancy armour in the world isn't going to give him bigger muscles."

Cleo led the cheering with a loud meow.

"Come on, Al!" Tom and Isis called out.

Percival snapped his visor shut.

Al raised the lance and stared straight ahead, looking determined.

"Charge!" King Arthur shouted.

The horses started to gallop towards one another. Clouds of dust billowed up under their thundering hooves. Tom watched as Al's lance came down.

The horses galloped closer and closer.

Al's face looked grim.

His lance made contact with Percival's breastplate...

Thunk!

Percival grunted. *Oof!* The air was literally knocked out of him as he tumbled off his horse and hit the ground.

Clank!

Al had won the first round.

"Hooray!" Tom and Isis cried.

The villagers started to cheer and whistle loudly.

"Second round!" bellowed King Arthur.

Al smiled and waved cautiously at the crowd. He swung Acorn round to begin the second charge. Acorn seemed unruffled, despite all the noise.

Percival's stallion, however, was not coping so well. The horse was wide-eyed and rearing up on its hind legs.

"Behave, you stupid beast!" Percival yelled at the stamping horse and kicked him with his spurs.

The horse whinnied. It pawed the ground, then reared up again. The weight of the lance pulled Percival out of the saddle and he landed on the ground with a clatter. The crowd started to laugh.

"Serves him right!" another peasant woman said.

Percival levered himself stiffly off the ground. Tom could see that his shining armour had been dented. Judging from his blazing-red cheeks, his pride had taken a knock too.

"You ridiculous animal!" Percival shouted at the horse. "Calm down, or I'll turn you into food for Father's hunting hounds."

King Arthur clapped his hands. "Leave the horse be. Come here, both of you," he said, beckoning Al and Percival forward. "There is no point in continuing the joust with that horse in such a state. Instead, you will both progress to the final and trickiest trial of all. This will be a true test of your valour."

"As you command, sire! I'm ready," Al said.

Underneath his short beard and moustache, King Arthur was smiling. "I have hidden a golden sword in a nearby cave," he said, with an air of mystery. "I challenge you both to seek it there. The man who finds it and returns it to me shall become my knight..." His blue eyes twinkled as he continued, "...but only if you can get past the dragons who are guarding it. What say you?"

"Dragons?" Percival scoffed. "Ha! Easy," he said, although Tom noticed his hands were shaking.

Al scratched his head and frowned. "Well, I've never met any dragons before. But I'll give it my very best shot, Your Royal Magnificence," he said, bowing low in front of King Arthur.

Tom turned to Isis. He was so desperate to

get the words out that he didn't really make sense. "Dragons! The riddle! Legend of the stone!"

Isis nodded eagerly. "Yes! Exactly! Everything in the riddle is coming true. King Arthur is the legend. I'm fairly certain my amulet is the stone in his sword. And Al's about to track the sword down in the *cavernous lair* full of dragons!"

She jumped up and down on the spot with such excitement that she trod on poor Cleo's tail. "Sorry, Fluffpot," she said. Snatching up the yowling cat, Isis smothered her in kisses.

"We're close now!" Tom said. "If good old Al finds King Arthur's sword, *we* can get the amulet!"

CHAPTER 6
THERE BE DRAGONS

"What's Percival playing at?" Isis asked, looking towards the horses, who were drinking thirstily from a stone trough.

Tom glanced over and saw Percival crouching by the side of Acorn. Percival looked over his shoulder with darting eyes. Al was standing on the other side of Acorn, stroking his nose and feeding him a handful of hay. He was so busy tending to the horse, he didn't notice his opponent's shifty behaviour.

"I don't know," Tom said. "Maybe he's adjusting his pants under his armour or something."

"I think he's up to no good," said Isis, heading over to warn Al. But there was no time.

Toot ta toot too TOOOOT!

King Arthur's servants sounded their horns and suddenly all eyes were on the king. He beamed at the villagers and then turned to Al and Percival.

"Stand by your horses," he said. "It is time for the race to begin!"

Tom waved at Al and gave him the thumbs up. "Good luck!" he shouted.

"Take your marks," King Arthur bellowed.

Al picked up Acorn's reins.

"Set..."

Percival smirked at Al in a way that made Tom's skin feel itchy.

"Go!"

Tom watched as Al wedged his muddy boot into Acorn's stirrup and started to heave himself up. But then the entire saddle slipped from the horse's back. Arms and legs flailing in the air, Al fell and landed in the mud with a *splat!*

The saddle landed on his head.

"Ouch! That's got to have **hurt**," said **one** of the villagers.

The wealthy villagers snig**gered with** delight, but the poorer ones s**houted** encouraging words to him.

"Come on, Al! Get back **on your horse,** lad!" someone called.

Tom and Isis rushed over **to him.**

"Are you OK?" Tom aske**d, pulling Al up** out of the mud.

Al picked up his saddle **and examined** the girth.

"The saddle must have co**me loose**," he said, shaking his head.

Tom and Isis exchanged a **knowing** glance.

"So *that's* what Percival was playing at," Tom said, helping Al fasten his saddle back on. "What a cheat."

91

The squire's son had already streaked off towards the cave in a cloud of kicked-up dust.

Al hauled himself back into the saddle.

"Move up," Isis said, vaulting on behind him.

"What are you doing?" Al asked.

"You didn't think we'd let you face this last trial alone?" she asked. "Plenty of room for three," she said, extending a hand to Tom. "Up you come," she said.

Tom looked nervous.

"I've only ever been on a donkey at the beach," he said.

Cleo, who had been twining herself around Acorn's legs, mewed loudly and pawed at Tom.

"Fluffpot thinks you're a scaredy cat."

Tom snorted half-heartedly, swallowed

hard and pulled himself up into the saddle behind them both.

"Your friends are going to be with you every step of the way, Al," he said. "We'll make sure Percival doesn't cheat again. Let's get going!"

"Friends! I got myself friends!" Al cried. "Good Lord, I'm a lucky lad."

They thundered away, with Cleo running alongside. Peering into the distance, Tom could barely see Percival now, he was so far ahead.

"How can we possibly catch up?" Tom shouted as the wind gusted in his face, almost taking his breath away.

Al glanced back at him. "He's on the road to the caves," he shouted. "But there's a shortcut."

"Where?" Isis asked.

Al pointed to their left. "The woods!"

They paused and stared into the dark woodland. The tree trunks were growing very close together, barely letting in any sunlight.

"We'll never get through there!" Tom said.

Al tapped his nose. "Trust me. There isn't an inch of countryside round here that Alymere, the pig-boy, doesn't know like the back of his hand."

They plunged into the shadowy woodland. Tom covered his eyes, convinced they were going to collide with a tree trunk at any moment.

But Al was right. There was a route through! Acorn picked his way nimbly over the mossy floor, moving more quickly than Tom thought possible. As the horse cantered

along, Cleo scampered at his side. Before
long, they shot out from the gloom of
the trees.

Ahead of them, Tom spied a massive, craggy rock face that loomed up in jagged points against the grey sky. It had lots of dark, house-sized holes.

"The caves!" he said.

"We've only gone and beaten Percival to it!" Al said, reining in Acorn behind a large boulder.

The three of them dismounted, then peered warily round the boulder. Outside the mouth of the largest cave stood two men, dressed head to toe in chainmail and carrying broadswords at their sides.

"They look like knights to me," Al said.

Over their chainmail shirts, Tom noticed that they wore red tunics with gleaming gold dragons on the front.

"Dragons!" Isis gasped.

"So *those* are the dragons King Arthur was talking about," Tom said. "See, Isis. I told you the fire-breathing ones weren't real."

Before Isis could respond, Al pulled her and Tom to the ground.

"Right," he said, squatting in the dust. "Tactics. We've got to get past those guards. So, what's the plan?"

Isis clasped a purring Cleo to her chest and pursed her lips. Tom scratched his head and found a pine cone tangled in his hair. Al wobbled a rotten tooth.

"Maybe we should just charge them," Tom said. "There's three of us and two of them."

"Not likely," Al said. "They're the king's knights! They'll mince us into sausage meat with those swords, faster than you can shout... er... pork chop."

"I know!" Isis said. "I've thought of a way to distract them. Then we can sneak in while they're in a muddle."

Tom tugged at the cone in his hair. "What are you going to do? Walk up there and ask them the way to Egypt? Or set Cleo on them?"

Cleo hissed and showed Tom her claws.

"Calm down, action cat! I was only joking," Tom said.

"Don't be silly," Isis said. "Cleo is going to be our lookout." Isis searched along the ground for a sharp stone. "Right, now watch this!" she said, holding up her slingshot, which she'd repaired. "The shoulder of the knight on the right. You see if I don't hit him dead on target."

She fired the stone towards the knight. It whistled through the air and caught him on the shoulder.

"Ha!" Isis said.

The knight cried out in pain. "Ow! Did you just throw something at me?" he said to his companion.

The second dragon knight shook his head. "Why would I do that?" he asked.

"Here," said Tom, quickly grabbing some pine branches and handing them to Isis and Al. "Camouflage."

"Camou-what?" asked Al.

"Use these branches as a disguise so that we blend in," explained Tom.

Isis fired another stone at the knight, this time hitting his left knee.

"Hey! Quit that!" said the injured knight.

"I *told* you, I didn't do anything!" said his friend.

As the two knights squabbled over the mysterious attack, Tom, Isis and Al darted out from behind their boulder. Holding the pine branches in front of them, they crept towards the cave and slipped inside. They made straight for the long, deep shadows at the back.

"It's very dark in here," Al whispered.

Tom blinked and stared into the gloom. The air was damp and cold. Suddenly, he noticed a golden glow much further into the cave.

"Do you see what I see?" Tom said, nudging Isis.

"I certainly do," she whispered.

CHAPTER 7
CAVING IN

"Cor, it's heavy," Al said, holding up the shining sword for Tom to see. "But it's not half pretty."

"It's brilliant," Tom said. "Solid gold, I bet."

As if under a spell, Isis carefully stroked the sparkling green amulet set into the base of the blade. "Yes, it is solid gold," she said, sighing longingly. "I should know – I used to have plenty of it."

Al swung the sword through the air. It made a satisfying swishing noise.

"I've never handled anything so grand before," he said. "Look at the hilt on it."

The carving on the hilt was impressive. Tom's heart fluttered and his mouth was suddenly dry with excitement.

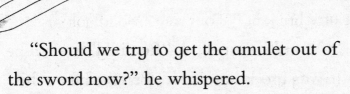

"Should we try to get the amulet out of the sword now?" he whispered.

"Good idea," Isis murmured. "But it'll be easier outside the cave where there's more light."

"Come on, Al," Tom called over. "Let's get back to the king with this."

Just as they started to make their way back through the cave, they heard a frantic yowling coming from outside.

"It's Fluffpot!" cried Isis. "Cleo's warning us that someone's coming!"

Sure enough, hooves clattered by the cave's entrance. These were followed by the sounds of swords clashing together. Next, footsteps thundered through the cave – coming closer, closer, closer. The sound bounced off the stone walls like hammers on an anvil.

"Oh no!" Tom said. "Percival!"

It was too late to hide. Percival drew his dagger and pointed it at them.

"Hand over the sword or I shall cut your throats!" Percival demanded, his nasty voice echoing through the cave.

Tom gulped. He looked at the gleaming, golden sword. He couldn't let Percival take the sword away from Al. Without the amulet, he and Isis would be stuck in King Arthur's England forever. But he also didn't fancy dying!

Tom wracked his brains to remember the skills he had learned at Atillus's gladiator school in Ancient Rome. Hadn't he fought bravely against the undefeated hero in the arena?

I've got to distract him — to wrong-foot him somehow, Tom thought. *Foot… feet… hmmm.*

He stared at Percival's fine boots – the ones he was so proud of. They were laced up to the knees, with tassels dangling from the front. *I know just the thing!* Tom thought.

"Look out!" Tom said, pointing at Percival's feet, "You're standing in a puddle!"

"My boots!" Percival yelped, looking down.

In that split second, Isis kicked the dagger out of Percival's hand.

Furious, Percival roared, "How dare you trick me!" He grabbed Tom and Isis by the scruffs of their necks and lifted them off the ground.

"Put those children down. Let's fight like men," Al cried, brandishing the golden weapon.

"No! Not until you give me the sword!" hissed Percival.

With her legs kicking out uselessly like a puppet, Isis cried, "Let go of me, you big lump!" She grabbed a handful of Percival's long hair and pulled until a clump came away in her hand.

Percival growled from the pain, but didn't loosen his iron grip.

Tom rummaged frantically through the facts, figures and memories in his mind for a good idea that would free them. He suddenly remembered something Percival had said in Al's hut.

"Aargh! A giant spider!" he shouted.

"What? Where?" shrieked Percival.

"On your head!" said Tom.

Percival dropped Tom and Isis and clasped his hands to his head. "Ugh! Get it off me!

I hate spiders!" Percival screamed and then dropped to the floor to retrieve his dagger. He turned on his heel and ran out of the cave.

"That was close," Tom said. "Percival's the biggest wimp I've ever met!"

Al clambered over the rocky floor. "Some gentleman he is," he scoffed. "Now let's go back to King Arthur."

But before they could leave the cave, the ground rumbled and the rocks beneath their feet started to crack.

"Here we go again," muttered Isis.

Tom watched open-mouthed as the crack in the ground travelled up through the rocky walls of the cave. In a shower of stones, Anubis's giant dog head appeared. The Egyptian god of the Underworld's red eyes shone angrily in the gloom.

"Oh no! You're joking. Not here!" Tom said.

Al fell to his knees and pressed the palms of his hands together. He stared at the pile of rocks, and with wide eyes began to pray.

"Dear Lord, I know I'm only a lowly pig-boy and not a fine nobleman, but please don't punish me for taking the sword," he whimpered. "I wasn't stealing. Honest!" He flung the golden sword across the cave, as if it was hot to the touch.

Tom ran over to him and put a reassuring hand on his shoulder. "Don't worry, Al," he said. "It's just a little earthquake. We will be fine."

Al looked up at him with desperate eyes. "No! I'm being punished for being too proud! I'm not worthy of being a knight." He started to pray loudly again. Then a small stone fell from the ceiling, bounced off his head and knocked him out cold.

Isis ran over to Al and shook him. "Are you OK? Wake up!"

"Leave the pig-boy alone! Pay attention to me!" Anubis boomed. A cloud of dust fell from the ceiling of the cave.

Tom glared up at the jackal-headed god. He was so annoyed at Anubis for ruining Al's efforts, and then hurting him, that he stamped his foot on the ground. "Look!" he said. "We've found the amulet – we just need to get it off the sword. And we'll do that as soon as we're out of the cave."

Anubis laughed in a creepy way that made the hair on Tom's arms stand up. "You'll never get out of here!" he shouted.

Tom felt his heart sink to the bottom of his boots.

"I'm going to teach you two a lesson you'll never forget," Anubis growled.

111

Suddenly, the whole cave began to shake violently. Rocks started to break free from the ceiling. They tumbled down the side of the cave.

"He's starting a rockslide!" Tom yelped.

"I hope you two like caves." Anubis's voice boomed beneath the roar of the falling rocks. "You'll be stuck here forever now. Don't bother screaming – nobody will hear you. HA HA HA!"

Tom watched in despair as the roof of the cave collapsed in a deafening downpour of stone and dust, blocking the exit and burying the golden sword. He coughed and waved his hand in front of his face. It was completely dark.

"Oh no!" Tom groaned. "Looks like we're trapped!"

CHAPTER 8
THE CAT'S MEOW

"Al!" shouted Tom, running over to his unconscious friend. "Can you hear me?"

Isis bent down and started slapping Al's cheeks. "Wake up!"

Al woke with a start. "Ow," he said, looking dazed and rubbing his head. "I had a terrible dream. I was being punished for stealing King Arthur's golden sword." He sat up and looked around the cave. "Oh no!

It wasn't a dream."

"Don't worry," said Tom. "It was just a rockslide. But we're going to get out of here."

"First we need to find the sword," said Isis.

As Tom's eyes adjusted to the dark, he spied the sword's carved handle sticking out from under a big boulder. But the blade was trapped beneath the rock. Tom pushed and pushed, but the stone wouldn't budge.

"Here, let me give you a hand," said Al, rising to his feet.

Together, Tom and Al pushed at the rock with their shoulders. Finally, the rock shifted slightly, and Isis was able to yank out the sword from under the rock.

"Good as new," she said, blowing dust off the shining blade and handing it to Al.

Tom gave Isis a thumbs up.

"He keeps
doing that," Isis told Al.
"Sticking his thumb in the air. I still
don't know what it means. Do you?"

"No," Al said. "But I think it means
something good."

Tom barely heard them. He was too

busy staring at the dazzling green amulet embedded in the sword's blade.

"We've got it," he said to Isis. "Now let's find a way out of here." All Tom and Isis needed to do was both touch the amulet and they would be whisked back to modern times. But he knew that there was no way Isis would leave without her pet cat. And besides, they'd promised to help Al. If they took the sword, he'd never get to become one of King Arthur's knights.

Isis, Tom and Al pushed and shoved at the huge rocks blocking the cave's entrance. Even when they all pushed together, they couldn't move them more than a few inches. But at least a bit of sunlight filtered through the cracks.

Isis paused to rub her back. "This is worse than being stuck in that statue," she muttered.

A faint meowing came in reply.

"That's right, Cleo," said Isis. "You know what I'm talking about… Wait a minute! Fluffpot?"

The meowing was definitely Cleo, but the noise sounded like it was coming from the back of the cave.

"There must be another way out!" Tom said excitedly.

Al nodded. "I've heard it told that these here caves have hidden tunnels."

Crawling about on their knees, they started to look for a different way out of the cave.

Tom patted the damp walls with his hands and found a narrow gap. He heard a meow – louder this time. "Guys! I've found it!" he called.

"Here we come, Fluffpot!" cried Isis.

117

Tom, Isis and Al crept through the tunnel's low, moss-covered walls. It was dank and cold, and their only guide through the dark was Cleo's meowing.

"This reminds me of home," Isis whispered to Tom. "The pyramids all had secret tunnels underneath them, to confuse tomb robbers."

Al was lagging behind; his height made crawling through the tunnel more difficult.

"Come on, Al," Tom urged. "It's not far now."

The tunnel gradually got wider, and the chink of light at the end got brighter and brighter. Finally, the three of them emerged, blinking, into the sunlight.

Cleo chased her tail and mewed loudly, as though she was celebrating.

"Well done, Fluffpot!" cried Isis, scooping

up her pet. "You saved us!"

"Thanks goodness!" exclaimed Al. "Let's go and get Acorn."

They walked back round to the front of the cave and peeped out from behind a bush, but the dragon knights were nowhere to be seen.

"Come on, the coast's clear," Tom said, and they headed over to the boulder Acorn was hidden behind. The horse was happily munching grass, and whinnied a greeting.

"Good boy, Acorn," called Al. "How do you fancy becoming a knight's trusty steed?"

A pair of shiny, tassled boots stepped out from behind a tree.

"Not so fast, pig-boy," said Percival, with a nasty smirk. He put one arm round Acorn's wide neck and in the other held his dagger.

"Hand over the sword, or Dobbin here is dinner for my father's hounds."

"Stop!" cried Al. "Don't hurt Acorn!" He approached Percival slowly, holding out the sword.

"No!" shouted Isis. "Don't let him have the sword. He doesn't deserve to win."

Al shook his head sadly. He handed the sword to Percival. "No, I couldn't do that to Acorn. He's been a true friend to me."

Al climbed on to Acorn's saddle and patted his shaggy mane. "I guess I wasn't meant to be a knight, after all," he said with a sigh. "I'll just be getting back to my pig sty, then." He buried his face in the horse's mane.

Percival danced round the forest clearing, swinging the sword. "Ooh! I'm going to buy a shiny new suit of armour. And a plumed helmet!" he laughed in delight. "All rise for dashing Sir Percival!"

"Sir Percival?" spat Tom in disgust. "More like Sir Cheatsalot!"

"Where I come from, we don't stand for cheating," said Isis. She loaded a pine cone

121

into her slingshot and pelted Percival. "Take that, you big bully!"

As Percival tried to dodge the steady storm of missiles being fired at him, Tom grabbed a large stick lying on the ground. He held it like a lance and charged.

"Hiiiiii-yaaaaaa!" Tom shouted, as he whacked Percival with the branch, taking him by surprise.

The golden sword flew out of Percival's hand, landing in the middle of the clearing.

Isis put two fingers in her mouth and whistled sharply. "Hey, Al!" she shouted. "Go get the sword."

Looking up, Al tapped his heels against Acorn's sides. The horse's tail swished, and he pawed at the ground with his hooves. Then he galloped into the clearing.

Percival ran to the sword, but the

carthorse was too fast – thundering along like he was in a race.

"Hooray!" cried Al, reaching down from his saddle and snatching up the sword with ease. He waved it in the air. "We did it!"

Just then, the two dragon knights stepped out from behind the trees. They applauded.

"Well done," said the first knight, raising the visor of his helmet. "Sir Galahad, it seems we have a deserving victor." He smiled at the other knight.

"Now let's take you back to the king," said the second knight. "Sir Gawain and I will ride as your bodyguards, in case Sir Cheatsalot gets up to any more tricks."

The knights mounted their horses, while Tom, Isis and Cleo climbed on to Acorn's saddle behind Al.

123

They left a furious Percival kicking the dirt in a fit of rage.

As they rode back to the village, Tom's mind raced. He was happy for his friend, but he knew there was no way they could get the amulet out of the sword with two Knights of the Round Table as guards.

They needed a new plan – and fast!

CHAPTER 9
ARISE, SIR AL

"Should we just grab the sword off Al and go?" Isis whispered in Tom's ear.

"We can't do that," Tom whispered back. "He won't get to be a knight if he doesn't return the sword."

"That's true," Isis said, sighing. "Oh well. We helped Al. Maybe when he's a knight, he'll be able to help us in return…"

Before they could come up with a better

plan, they arrived back at the clearing, where excited villagers cheered their return.

"Are you sure I'm not dreaming?" said Al, shaking his head.

"It's not a dream, Al – you really did it," said Tom, giving his friend a pat on the back. "You're going to be a knight!"

The two dragon knights stood next to the king, speaking softly in his ear. Every now and then, King Arthur nodded. Tom watched their lips moving. The cheering villagers drowned out most of what was said but he did pick out 'calm, brave and kind'.

King Arthur gestured for Al to come over to him.

"Wish me luck," Al gulped.

Al placed the golden sword in King Arthur's hand. Tom and Isis exchanged worried looks. Once again, the amulet was out of their reach.

King Arthur sniffed at Al and frowned. "Normally I'd insist you have a good bath first."

Al looked down at his muddy clothes. "Sorry, Your Royal Highness."

"No matter!" King Arthur said brightly. "You are pure of soul, if not of body. Now, kneel before me, young Alymere."

Al knelt. The crowd gasped as King Arthur stood and drew his sword. A scared-looking Al clutched at his neck and stumbled backwards.

"Please spare me, Your Kingliness. I'm right fond of my head."

"*Is* he going to chop off his head?" Isis asked, clutching Cleo close to her. "Don't look, Fluffpot," she whispered, covering Cleo's eyes with her hand.

"Of course not!" Tom said. "It's fine. Watch!"

The smiling King Arthur ordered Al to kneel back down again. He lowered the flat of the gold sword on to Al's right shoulder. Then he moved the sword over his head to his left shoulder and gently touched him there too.

"I dub you a Knight of the Realm of King Arthur!" the king said. "Arise, Sir Alymere!"

Tom chuckled when Al stood and faced the crowd. He had the biggest smile Tom had ever seen.

Al gave a bow. The villagers cheered and clapped.

"Go on, Al! We knew you had it in you!"

"That's our knight, that is! Good old Al!" But Tom's spirits were dampened when he heard a few mean comments from the richer villagers.

A man who looked like an older version of Percival shouted, "Ridiculous! How could the king make this stinking pig-boy a knight?"

Tom looked over at King Arthur and wondered if he had heard the nasty remarks. Sure enough, the king held his sword high. Everyone's cheering dropped away to silence.

"Shame on *you* for not knowing better!" said King Arthur. "Call yourselves noblemen? Riches and fancy clothes do not make a good knight.

"A knight must have special qualities," the king continued. "Bravery, above all! Young Al... *Sir* Alymere, here, showed how brave he is. He fought men much older than him, on horses far superior to his. He did not flinch. He did not run."

Al blushed and looked at the ground.

"And a knight must show manners and courtesy," King Arthur said. "Why, when the squire's son, Percival, caused a lady to drop her basket of eggs, I saw for myself how Alymere helped her."

Percival's friends and family started to grumble.

But King Arthur bellowed, "QUIET!" and they fell silent.

The king turned back to the crowd. "Sir Alymere has proven that he has all the values of a knight. He should be an example to you all."

Then King Arthur handed Al the golden sword with the green amulet embedded in the blade. "You will need a weapon worthy of a knight, Sir Alymere. Take this sword and use it to serve your king and country."

Al, holding his golden sword, was carried around the village on the blacksmith's shoulders. The villagers' applause was deafening.

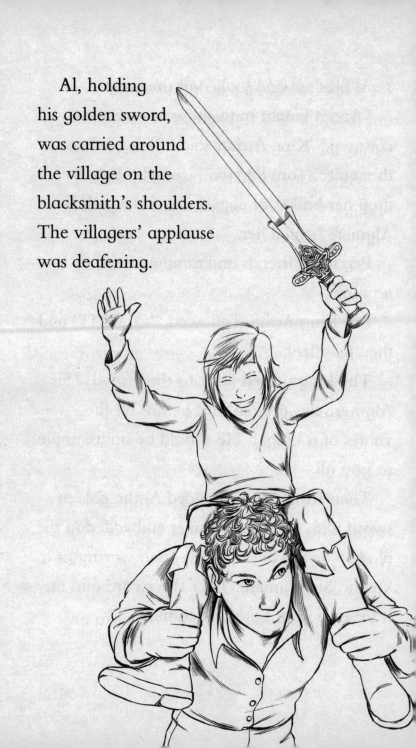

"Feast! We shall feast tonight and toast our local hero!" the blacksmith shouted, setting Al down.

"Aye!" the washerwoman said. "Come along, ladies. We owe it to our champion, Alymere, to bake, stew and fry a meal fit for the king."

As the delighted villagers started to drift away to prepare for the celebration of Al's knighthood, tears started to stream down the boy's dirty cheeks.

"Are you all right?" Tom asked.

Al wiped his face with his sleeve. "I just can't believe how lucky I am," he said. "Thank you so much for your help, my friends. You're great fighters, both of you. And very brave."

Isis sighed happily. "Yes, I am."

"Maybe I could ask King Arthur to give

133

you another go at being a knight?"

A grin started to spread across Tom's face. He was tempted for a moment. He thought about charging through the woods on a horse, jousting in a tournament, and meeting all the Knights of the Round Table.

Calm down and stop being stupid, he told himself. *I don't belong in this time.*

But Tom simply couldn't stop thinking about what a great guy King Arthur seemed to be. *I wouldn't mind fighting for him. Being a medieval knight would be a whole load better than school!*

When he looked over at Isis and Cleo, however, he remembered that they would never get into the Afterlife without his help. And of course he would miss Mum with her comfy hugs and silly jokes. Then there was Dad, with his stories about the Ancient

Greeks and Romans and Egyptians. *Well, I suppose I might miss them a bit...*

"It's brilliant of you to offer," Tom said, sighing heavily. "But no thanks. We'll leave the knightly deeds to you, Sir Alymere."

"Well, I feel I should repay you somehow," Al said.

"Actually," said Isis, staring at Al's shiny golden sword. "There is one little, teeny tiny thing you could do for us…"

"Of course, my lady," said Sir Alymere, bowing deeply. "You only have to ask."

"That lovely green stone," Isis said, pointing to the amulet. "It would look so pretty as a necklace." She fluttered her eyelashes.

"It is yours, my lady," said Al, gallantly handing her the gleaming sword. The amulet sparkled a bright, vivid green.

Isis eagerly grabbed the sword and tried to dig the amulet out with her fingernails. "Get out, you stupid thing!" she said through gritted teeth. But the amulet wouldn't budge.

Cleo wound herself round her mistress's legs, purring loudly.

"Good idea, Cleo!" Isis said, sucking her sore fingers. "You have a go!"

The cat dug her little claws under the glittering jewel. Finally, the amulet came loose. Isis grabbed it and held it up to the light.

"Thank you, Al," said Isis. "You've been a true friend and a real gentleman."

"But wait! Aren't you going to stay for the feast?" asked Al.

"Sorry, Sir Al. We've really got to be moving on," said Tom. "But good luck fighting the Saxons!"

Tom, Isis and Cleo ran to the edge of the clearing. They stood in a little triangle.

"Here, Tom, give me your hand and take Cleo's paw," said Isis. "Hurry!"

When they all touched the amulet, it began to glow. As the green light spread, wind whipped round their ankles. Growing stronger, it swirled through the meeting place, where King Arthur sat in his carved chair, flanked by his mighty knights, and villagers bustled about preparing for a feast.

Tom felt a familiar sucking sensation as the scene in front of him started to blur.

"Here we go!" he said, squeezing his eyes shut as they were whisked through the tunnels of time to the future.

CHAPTER 10
BACK TO SCHOOL

Tom landed on his bottom with a thump. Opening his eyes, he saw that he was behind the art block – all signs of King Arthur and his knights had vanished. Isis and Cleo were sprawled next to him on the ground. Now they were back, her bronze skin had been replaced by the crusty yellow wrappings of a five-thousand-year-old mummy.

"Oh, bother," said Isis, poking her bandages in dismay.

"Cheer up! We've got another amulet," Tom said brightly.

Isis held the glittering jewel in her bandaged hand. "I suppose that's true," she said with a grin. "Two down, four to go!"

That reminded Tom of something. He checked his watch. "Same date and time as when we left!" he said. Then he frowned. "Oh no! That means I've got double Maths next! I hope Anubis comes for the amulet before the bell rings. Double Maths is bad enough without a bad-tempered Egyptian god shouting at me."

"Maybe he won't bother," Isis said cheerfully. "Maybe the old dog has decided that since we've done such a great job, he will just let me kee—"

The sky suddenly darkened and a gale blew up. The branches of the tree next to the art block started to wave wildly, as if a hurricane was sweeping through the playground.

"Spoke too soon," muttered Tom.

The ground began to rumble and shake,

and then the enormous jackal-headed god
burst through the wall of the art block. He
walked towards Tom and Isis menacingly.

"Hand over my amulet, you greedy
little girl," barked the god angrily,
spraying specks of spit on Tom and Isis.

"Ugh. Say it, don't spray it," said Isis, wiping the dribble off her arm.

"I see you still haven't learned anything, Princess Isis," sneered Anubis.

"Actually, I've learned that a pig-boy can be braver and more gallant than a nobleman," said Isis. "So there!" She stuck out her tongue.

Tom shook his head in dismay. Isis might have learned that having a title doesn't make someone better than everyone else – but she couldn't seem to get it through her head that being rude to the Egyptian god of the Underworld was a bad idea. Though of course her brains *had* been sucked out through her nose when she was mummified...

"I will teach you to respect your betters!" raged Anubis, his red eyes flashing. "You will give me the amulet now, or I'll send you

straight back to King Arthur's England.
I believe there's a vacancy for a pig-girl!"

"All right, all right. Don't get your
loincloth in a twist," Isis said grumpily,
dropping the sparkling amulet into the
god's hand.

"Good call," whispered Tom. "I can't
really see you as a pig-girl."

Anubis stalked round the children, like
a jackal circling his prey. Tom felt an icy
chill run up his spine as the god of the dead
brushed past him. Cleo whimpered and
pawed at Isis, her tail sticking straight up
and quivering with fear. Only Isis didn't
look scared.

"Your first two adventures have been
nothing but a warm up," bellowed Anubis.
"But I'm through with this child's play." He
smiled nastily, baring his sharp, yellow teeth.

"Your next challenge will be full of peril and will take you to the most dangerous time in hist—"

Whump!

A football smacked Anubis right in the face. In a flash, the god disappeared.

Tom's friend Danny came running to collect his ball.

"Sorry about that, mate," said Danny. "Hope it didn't hit you."

"Nope," said Tom. "It didn't get *me*."

Just then the bell rang. Tom walked back into school with Danny. From behind him, Tom heard Isis say, "I think I'll take a nap, Fluffpot. This finding-amulets business is tiring."

Phew! thought Tom. *At least I won't be distracted by Isis in this class.*

As he walked to his Maths lesson, Tom

thought about the adventure he'd just had. The jousts and the swordfights, the shining armour and the magnificent horses. Sure he'd been clonked with a lance and nearly crushed by a rockslide – but he'd learned how to fight like a knight. And best of all, he'd got to meet King Arthur! Now he knew that this legendary hero wasn't just a myth – he'd seen him with his very own eyes.

Tom smiled as he sat down at a desk. *Four more amulets to find*, he mused. *I wonder where the third one will be hidden…*

And as Mr Braintree scribbled maths problems on the whiteboard, Tom started dreaming about other legendary leaders. Who would he meet next?

Tom glanced over and saw Isis lying on the carpet in the reading corner. Cleo was curled up next to her, already fast asleep. He smiled. An Egyptian princess could be a handful – but he had to admit they made a great team!

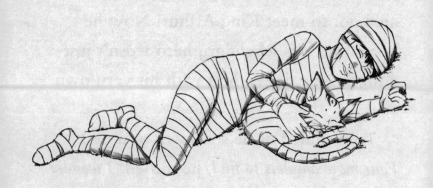

TURN THE PAGE TO . . .

→ Meet the REAL knights!

→ Find out fantastic FACTS!

WHO WERE THE MIGHTIEST KNIGHTS?

Find out more about the legendary King Arthur and his brave Knights of the Round Table.

KING ARTHUR was a legendary king. As a young man he proved himself the rightful King of England by pulling a magical sword out of a stone. Arthur was then given his own special sword, called Excalibur. During his reign he married the beautiful Guinevere, built a magnificent castle called Camelot, and created the Knights of the Round Table, an order made up of the kingdom's twelve best knights.

LANCELOT was one of King Arthur's most famous knights, known for his bravery and good looks. He was invited to join the Knights of the Round Table when he convinced one of King Arthur's enemies to surrender without a fight! King Arthur trusted Lancelot more than any of his other knights, but that turned out to be a BIG mistake. Lancelot fell in love with Queen Guinevere and stole her away from King Arthur. But Lancelot regretted his actions, and ended his life a hermit, feeling guilty for betraying his friend, till the end of his days.

GAWAIN was King Arthur's nephew. The most famous story about Gawain is of him and the Green Knight, who challenged Gawain to chop off his head, as long as he could do the same to Gawain a year later. Not believing this was possible, Gawain beheaded him, but the Green Knight simply picked his head up and stuck it back on! For the next year, Gawain was always worried and wore a magical green ribbon around his neck, which protected him from the Green Knight's axe.

GALAHAD was Lancelot's son, known for his courage. Like King Arthur, Galahad pulled a sword out of a stone, proving that he was the knight destined to find the Holy Grail, which was a sacred cup. Along with two other Knights of the Round Table – Bors and Percivale – Galahad went on a long, difficult quest to find the Holy Grail. When he finally found it, Galahad was so happy that he asked to die in that very moment!

WEAPONS

The Knights of the Round Table were very brave. They defended England against invaders and always fought with honour and courage. To help them defeat their enemies they used lots of different weapons.

Mace: cheap and easy to make, but also deadly. It had a round head made from stone, iron, bronze or steel and it was covered in sharp spikes.

Halberd: a lethal weapon. It had the head of an axe on top of a pike, which was a long wooden pole.

Lance: a long pole with a sharp metal point, used by knights on horseback. In jousting tournaments, the point would be replaced with something blunt, so that it could be used to knock an opponent off his horse.

Flail: used by knights and foot soldiers. It had a short wooden handle with a spiky metal ball attached to it by a chain, so that it could be swung round.

Sword: only used by knights as they were expensive to make. A double-edged sword called the broadsword was used in combat.

FANTASTIC FACTS

Impress your friends with these facts about Medieval England!

➤ The Battle of Hastings in 1066 didn't actually take place in Hastings; it took place at Senlac Hill which is six miles away from Hastings.

That's as far as the Isle of Wight is from the coast of England.

➤ In Medieval Law animals could be charged with committing a crime. They were tried in court and given sentences for injuring or killing people and even stealing.

They must have been barking mad!

➔ During 1348–49, a third of England's population died from the Black Death. No one knew it was caused by rats carrying infected fleas. Many people thought it was a punishment from God. It was also thought that bathing and changing your clothes would make God angry, as it was a sign that you cared too much about what you looked like. So lots of people didn't wash. *Stinky!*

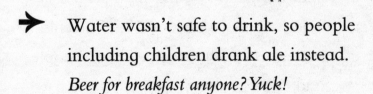

➔ Water wasn't safe to drink, so people including children drank ale instead. *Beer for breakfast anyone? Yuck!*